To

Caio

Merry Christmas

This book is dedicated to my son Shaun who has made losing things into an artform, and Faith who has brought the book to life with her illustrations, thank you.

Where do lost thing's go?

Written by

Simon Allen

Illustrations by

Faith Broomfield-Payne

Have you ever wondered, where do the lost things go?

Are they hidden in a draw somewhere, or behind the bedroom door.

Do they change their **shape** somehow, or slip on a **Disguise**. Are they waiting for the moment to **pounce** and

SHOUT...

Are they moved when you are sleeping, by invisible house elves,

To dark and dusty corners,

On out of reach top shelves,

Or does a furry monster, Creep into our bedrooms,

Eating all our bits and bobs,

as though they were mushrooms,

Do they peep from behind my wardrobe,

Or

Giggle in my bed,

Are they snuggled up all nice and warm,

Among my pants and socks,

Have they made it to the
bottom, of a forgotten
old toy box.

Some **bobby pins**, a **Light** up pen, My **blankey** and my **hat**.

My best friend, a ***RAGGY*** doll,

Tippy my old **cat,**

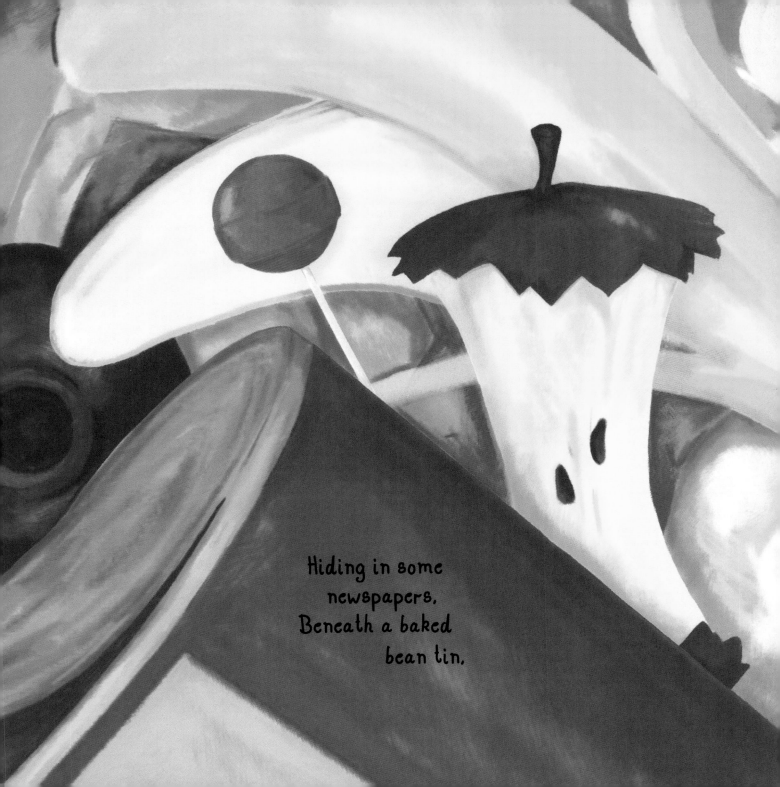

Hiding in some
newspapers,
Beneath a baked
bean tin.

I'd like to think a **fairy,**
has gathered them
all up.

And keeps them till I need them most,

In a giant

buttercup,

Where they are, we can only guess,
For the truth we do not know.
But wouldn't it be great to find ...

Where all the Lost Things Go

the end

Printed in Great Britain
by Amazon